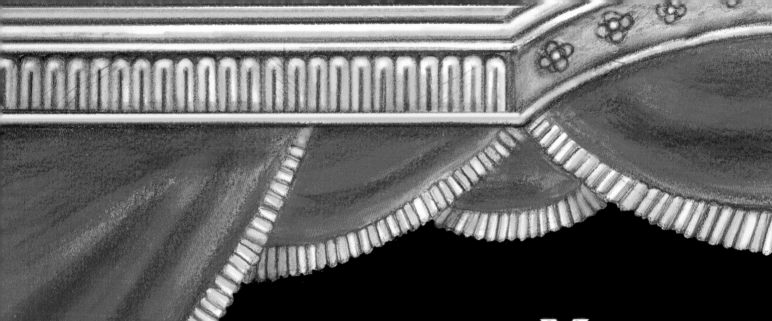

MARC

The MOVIE

Written by

LIZ HOCKINSON

ELLO

MOUSE

Illustrated by
KATHRYN OTOSHI

When the lights came down and shadows flickered on the silver screen, Marcello crouched under a plush seat in the Grand Palazzo Theatre. There he nibbled on popcorn dropped from crunchy bags and gooey candy stuck to the floor. He watched movies over and over until the final credits rolled.

As the velvet curtain closed, he scampered home to a little hole in the wall.

"Marcello Mousetriani, you're late for dinner again."

"Oh Mama," said Marcello, "I watched the greatest movie."

"My little dreamer," sighed Mama.
"Eat, eat. You're the tiniest mouse I've ever seen."

She pushed a plate of steaming spaghetti across the table.

"Movies, movies, movies," said Papa.
"You must scavenge for cheese like other mice."

But Marcello knew he was not like other mice.

Movies played in his head and stories stirred in his heart.

The next morning, he got up early to gather tidbits of cheese

at the Parmesan factory. He tiptoed past Ravioli, the theatre cat.

The cat's sharp teeth glistened in the sun.

PARMESAN
FACTORY

After a hard day at work, Marcello still went to the movies every night. Sometimes he scrambled up the wall, flattened out like a pancake, and slipped under the ledge to the projection booth. He watched Roberto, the projectionist, mount large reels of film and thread the enormous projector. The sound of film spinning was music to Marcello's ears.

By watching movies, he learned how lighting created mood, editing told the story, and music made the audience laugh and cry. The more Marcello learned about movies, the more he loved them.

One night after a hard day of scavenging, Marcello climbed to the rooftop of the Grand Palazzo Theatre. He gazed at the vast sky above. The stars in the Milky Way looked like the stream of light from the projector to the silver screen.

"I am so tiny, but my dream is so big," he said.

That night, as Mama kneaded pizza dough and Papa sat in his easy chair reading the newspaper, Marcello announced, "I want to make a movie."

Mama shook her head in wonder. Bernardo and Sofia rolled over laughing.

"That's a big job for such a little mouse," said Papa.

When Mama tucked Marcello in bed he said, "I love movies more than anything."

"Come with me," whispered Mama.

They scurried up a winding banister to a quiet, dusty attic. In a corner stood a movie camera covered with spider webs.

"Follow your heart, Marcello," Mama said.

From that day on Marcello filmed everything he saw: Mama hanging wash out the

window to dry, Sophia and Bernardo fighting over chocolate biscotti at breakfast,

Papa shaving his mouse-stash, and hundreds of hungry mice at the factory. Marcello

practiced framing shots, taking close ups, and shooting a montage.

Marcello knew he had a story to tell. So he wrote a screenplay over and over until he got writer's cramp in his paw.

He advertised in the *Rodent Gazette* for a swing gang. Able-bodied mice went to work hammering and painting to build a set. Marcello shouted into a megaphone, "This mice-en-scene must be the best ever!"

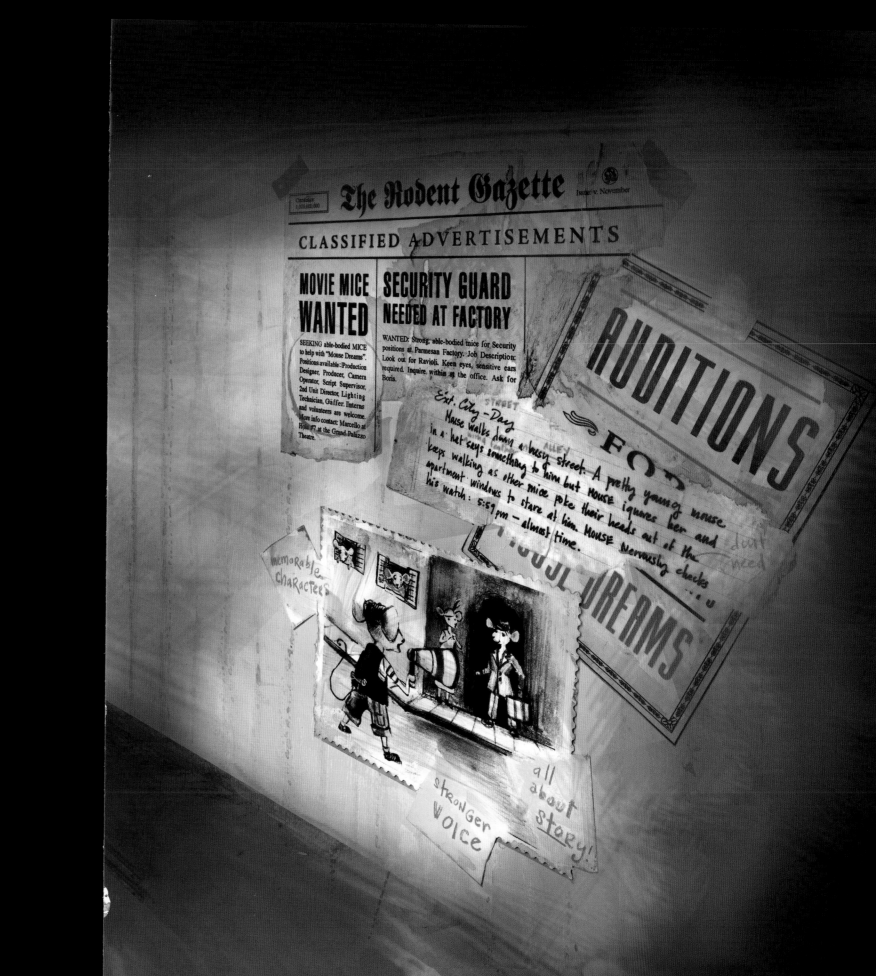

He plastered posters over mouse holes everywhere. Mice spread the word, whispering mouth to mouse. Mice from all over the city formed a long line to audition.

When Sergio the theatre manager saw this, he became furious. "No mice allowed in my theatre," he yelled. *THWAP, THWAP*, he swatted his broom. "*Gatto, gatto!* Where is that fat cat when I need him?"

At that moment, Ravioli zipped around the corner and pounced. Marcello escaped by a whisker.

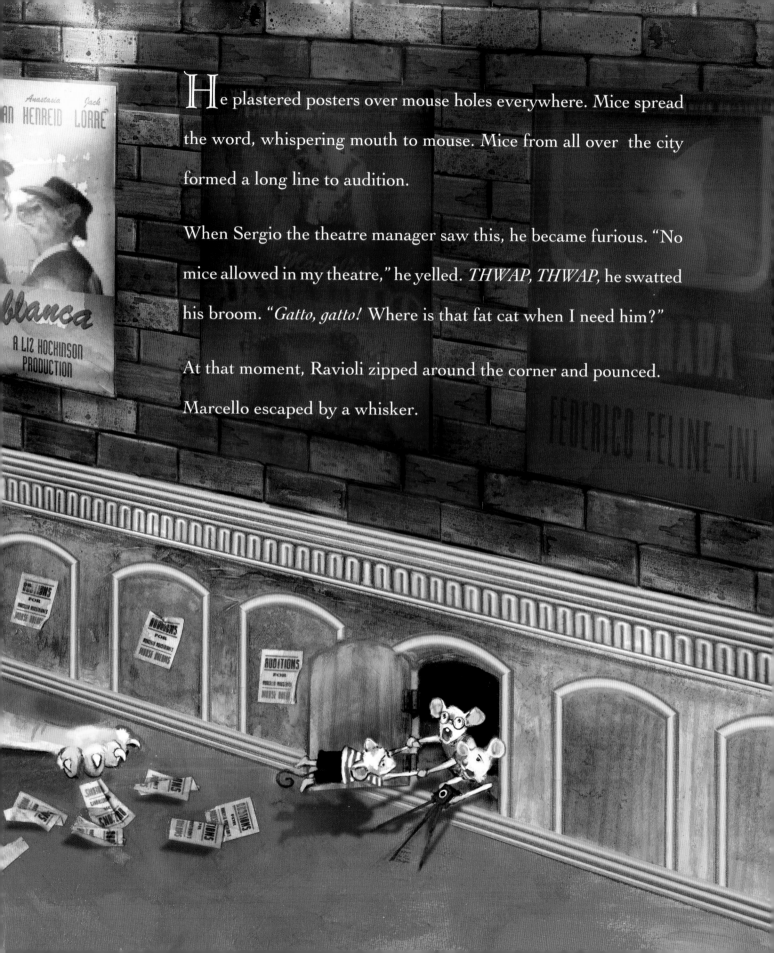

So Marcello ushered mice in under the back door. Some mice danced, some mice sang, some mice recited parts from the script. Finally all the cast members were chosen except one: the villain.

"I'll have to begin shooting anyway," said Marcello. He adjusted the camera for the opening scene. "Quiet on the set." The actors took their places. The clapboard came down with a *WHACK*. "Scene one, take one. Action!" yelled Marcello.

Suddenly, Ravioli flew through the air, his claws stretched out like daggers.

"Noooooooooo!" squeaked Marcello, as mice scrambled for their lives.

But the camera kept rolling. Looking through the lens, Marcello focused. He zoomed.

He dollied. "Cut!" yelled Marcello. "That's it! That's wonderful! That's a take!"

Ravioli stopped in his tracks. "What? You're filming me?"

"You're a natural," said Marcello.

"*Rowl,*" meowed Ravioli. "I can see my name in lights now."

When winter came, fluffy flakes of snow covered the ground, making food harder to find. Even the cheese factory closed down. So Marcello had to forage all day and film all night.

Sometimes the hungry film crew didn't show up, so Marcello had to do their jobs too. "I won't stop production no matter what," he said.

One night, Marcello was so tired that he fell asleep in his bowl of thin minestrone soup, and Papa carried him to bed.

MOUSE DREAMS

ADMISSION: Adults: 2 Chunks of Cheese
Children: 1 Chunk of Cheese

NOW PLAYING
Mouse Dreams

NOW PLAYING
Mouse Dreams

B ut Marcello never gave up.

Mouse Dreams premiered a few months later.
Mice stood in line for hours to get tickets.

"My son, the movie mouse," said Papa, patting
Marcello on the back.

Marcello glowed from the tip of his ears to
the tip of his tail.

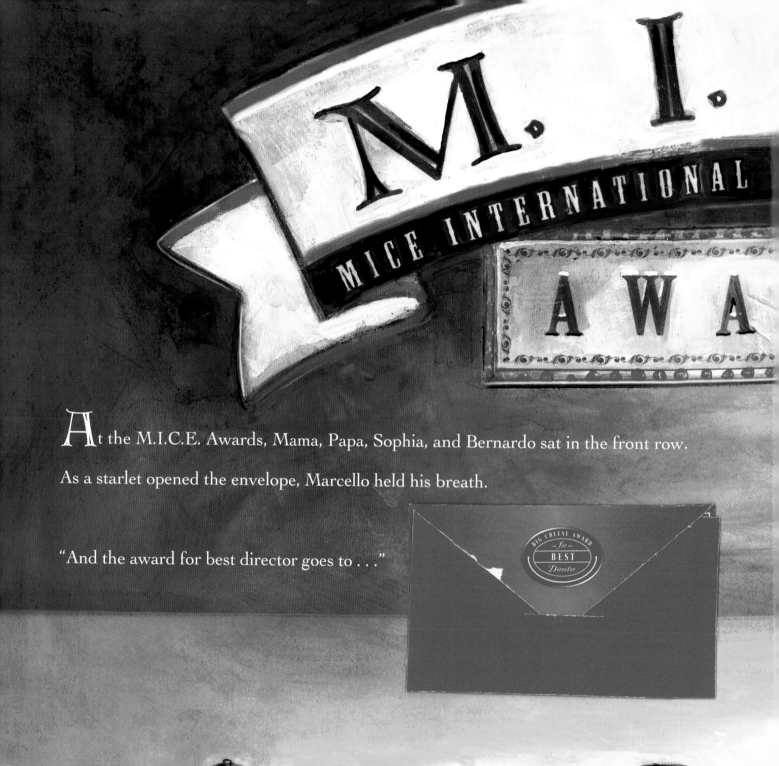

At the M.I.C.E. Awards, Mama, Papa, Sophia, and Bernardo sat in the front row.

As a starlet opened the envelope, Marcello held his breath.

"And the award for best director goes to . . ."

BIG CHEESE AWARD
— for —
BEST
Director

"Bravo, bravo!" the audience cheered. Marcello's family clapped louder than anyone.

"I want to thank my Mama and my Papa," said Marcello. "And of course the great actor, Ravioli."

"*EEEEEEEEK!*" shrieked the audience as the huge cat strutted to the stage.

But Ravioli just tipped his top hat.

Cameras flashed. The paparazzi shouted, "Say cheese!"
Marcello and Ravioli grinned.

THE END

Fine

That's a Wrap!

~*Follow Your Dream*~

It takes courage and a strong will to follow your dream. Marcello followed his, but it wasn't easy! Did you know that even some of our most talented and successful movie directors had to face their fears and start somewhere? Here's what they have to say to you:

ANDREW STANTON
Director of *Finding Nemo;* co-director of *Bug's Life*

When I was a young movie mouse I learned the very same lessons:
find a story you're dying to tell, capture the images of your mind's eye on camera,
and turn every villainous cat into an advantage.

GEORGE LUCAS
Director of the *Star Wars* Episodes

If you want to be successful in a particular field of endeavor, I think perseverance is one of the
key qualities. It's very important that you find something that you care about, that you have a
deep passion for, because you're going to have to devote a lot of your life to it.

GEORGE MILLER
Director of *Babe: Pig in the City*

We love telling each other stories. They are almost as important to us as eating and breathing.
Making movie stories involves team work, organization, drawing and designing, writing words and
speaking them, making sets, costumes and props, and weaving together pictures, sounds and ideas.
It is sometimes very difficult but always enormous fun.

~ *Movie Mouse Glossary* ~

CAST: The actors chosen to be in a movie.

CLAPBOARD: A small hinged chalkboard that is snapped shut to mark the beginning of filming.

CLOSE-UP: A close shot of a person or object that fills an entire frame.

CREDITS: The list of actors, crew, and everyone who helped make the movie.

CUT: The command that a director gives to end the filming of a scene.

DIRECTOR: The person who guides the actors, the action, and the filming to create a movie.

DOLLY: To move the camera along on a wheeled platform while filming.

EDIT: To splice, trim, and arrange shots in order to create a finished movie.

FOCUS: To adjust the camera lens so that the picture looks sharp and clear.

MISE-EN-SCENE *(Mice-en-Scene):* The atmosphere and mood of a movie.

MONTAGE: A series of shots edited together to create a mood or show the passage of time.

PRODUCTION: The phase of movie-making during which filming takes place.

PROJECTOR: A machine that shines light through spinning film to show moving pictures.

SCRIPT: The written version of a movie describing the scenes, characters, action, and dialogue.

SET: The area, often a decorated sound stage, where the action takes place during filming.

SHOT: A single, constant recording made by a movie camera.

STARLET: A young, soon-to-be famous actress.

SWING GANG: The carpenters, painters, and decorators who build and take down the set.

TAKE: A performance or scene filmed in one shot.

WRAP: The successful conclusion of filming.

ZOOM: To adjust the camera lens so that the subject appears closer in the frame.